NICKY

First published in Great Britain by Andersen Press Ltd in 1997
First published in Picture Lions in 1998
1 3 5 7 9 10 8 6 4 2
ISBN: 0 00 664650-6

Picture Lions is an imprint of the Children's Division,
part of HarperCollins Publishers Ltd, 77-85 Fulham Palace Road, Hammersmith, London W6 8JB
Text and illustrations copyright © Tony Ross 1997
The author/illustrator asserts the moral right to be identified as the author/illustrator of the work
A CIP catalogue record for this title is available from the British Library.
Printed and bound in Singapore by Imago

NICKY

Tony and Zoë Ross

PictureLions

An Imprint of HarperCollinsPublishers

"I'm not going to go to school!"

"It'll be nice."

"No, it won't. I won't know anybody."

"You'll soon make friends."

"School dinners will make me sick."

"No, they won't. School dinners are lovely."

"Marcia says the teachers will bite me."

"No, they won't. They'll tell you exciting things."

"I'm not going to go in! I'll be the littlest."

"Everybody is little. They'll love you."

"Well, what was it like?"

"Wonderful! Dinner was great, I wasn't the littlest,

and I made a new friend called Nicky."

"That's nice."

"Nicky has lovely hair."

"Sweet."

"Sometimes Nicky is a bit naughty..."

"Mmmm!"

"...but has a lovely smiley face."

"Ahhh!"

"Nicky wears LOADS of pink..."

"Peachy!"

"...and is very strong."

"Wow!"

"Can Nicky come to tea? And stay for a sleepover?"

"Of course, and you can go to school together tomorrow."

"Tomorrow? You mean we have to go again tomorrow?"